No Biting!
by Karen Katz

Grosset & Dunlap
An Imprint of Penguin Group (USA) Inc.

ISBN 978-0-448-45581-5   10 9 8 7 6 5 4 3

No biting your friends!
What can you bite?

Apples!

No hitting Mommy!
What can you hit?

A drum!

No pushing in line!
What can you push?

A swing!

No kicking the dog!
What can you kick?

A ball!

No spitting at your brother!

When can you spit?

When you brush your teeth!

Can you remember?

Yes, I can!

$4.99 US
($5.99 CAN)

No hitting Mommy! What can you hit?

A DRUM!

Your little one will love learning to say NO to hitting—and biting and pushing and kicking and spitting—and YES to nice manners! This book comes with a sheet of stickers for added fun.

Grosset & Dunlap
www.penguin.com/youngreaders
Ages 3 and up

The books in this series are listed inside. Collect them all!

ISBN 978-0-448-45581-5

EAN

50499>

9 780448 455815